I0674670

Young Heroes Collection

Vol. 3

YOUNG HEROES

COLLECTION

VOL. 3

DICK SHAND

Edited by Austin Mardon, Catherine Mardon
& Tom Shand

GM

PRESS

Copyright © 2022 by Austin Mardon

All rights reserved. This book or any portion thereof may not be reproduced or used in any manner whatsoever without the express written permission of the publisher except for the use of brief quotations in a book review or scholarly journal.
First Printing: 2022

Typeset and Cover Design by Celine Trinidad

Print ISBN: 978-1-77369-836-6
ebook ISBN: 978-1-77369-845-8

Golden Meteorite Press
103 11919 82 St NW
Edmonton, AB T5B 2W3
www.goldenmeteoritepress.com

Contents

Introduction

Most of the YOUNG HERO stories have been read by nine-year-old students at Willow Park Elementary School who needed help in their reading skills. Students who were in Grade 3 from 1991 to 1996 will remember many of these stories.

We acted some of them out in the classroom. Every kid wanted a leading role. In 1996, I met a young girl who had a role in a story in 1993. She came over to greet me and recalled the exact role she had and the name of the story.

YOUNG HERO stories and GRANDPA'S BEDTIME STORIES (generally for younger students) were also acted out at the following schools:

Chinook Park Elementary School, Calgary, AB.

Canyon Meadows Elementary School, Calgary, AB.

Cliff Rd. Public School, Tsawwassen, B.C.

Also the E.S.L. (English Second Language) students at the Y.W.C.A in Calgary acted out several of these stories.

Storyteller and Writer
DICK SHAND

A Flaming Experience

CALINE COULDN'T SLEEP. She was suffering from after-shock. Her little body was trembling in the motel bed that she shared with her young sister Miranda. During the fire she had been fairly calm, but now that the danger was past frightening memories haunted her. Her lungs still burned from the smoke, and the back of her legs tingled from the heat of the flames that had been ever so close.

Her mind kept replaying the terrifying events. Her mom, her sister Miranda, and she slept under their small two storey wooden frame house. Her dad was on night shift. The smell of the smoke woke her up. She went to the top of the stairs and saw flames at the foot of her staircase. She rushed to wake her mom and Miranda. There was no escape down the stairs. The only exit was out of one of the bedroom windows.

From the window in her room there was a long drop to the ground, but in her mother's room there was a short drop to a small peaked roof over the front door. She thought, "If we can slide out onto the roof, we can get to the ground."

Caline's mother was afraid of heights. She didn't like the

idea of jumping out a window. Caline knew there was no choice. She could hear the flames crackling, and the smoke was getting thicker. She opened the window and pushed out the screen. Then she threw two pillows out the window for a cushion to land on and tied a sheet to the leg of the bed.

"You'll have to go first," she said to her mother. "Hang on to the sheet and you can slide down onto the roof over the front door. Then I'll hand Miranda down to you."

Her mother said, "I can't! I'm afraid! I'm afraid!"

"Be brave and show us how," Caline said encouragingly.

Her mother gingerly put one leg over the window sill. She knew if she looked at the ground she would get dizzy. She kept her eyes level with the window.

Caline put the end of the sheet in her mother's hands. She helped her mother lift the other leg over the sill and made sure her mother had a strong grip on the sheet; then Caline helped her mother over the window sill and made sure she could slide down the twisted sheet to the roof.

"I'm touching the roof," her mother called up breathlessly. The roof was only about five feet below the window sill, but to her it seemed like a hundred.

"Great!" replied Caline. "Now plant both feet firmly. I'm going to lower Miranda down to you."

Caline could feel the heat on her back. Flames were at the door of the bedroom. There was little time to waste. She picked up Miranda and slid her over the window sill and down to her mother's outstretched arms.

"Sit down and make room for me," she shouted.

Before Caline climbed out the window, she tied a second sheet to the first one as they needed help in getting from the porch roof to the ground. It was a long jump to the ground, and she didn't want anyone to get hurt.

Flames had now entered the room. Caline didn't hesitate. She climbed over the window sill and slid down the sheet until she touched the porched roof. She joined her mother and sister on the small, pitched roof twelve feet above the ground. The next step was to slide down off the roof to the grass below using the second sheet to help them part of the way.

"We have to slide down the sheet as far as we can go and then drop on the pillows," she explained to her mother. "You have to go first so you can catch Miranda. I'll carry her on my back when I come down."

She got her mother to lie down on the roof and push her feet over the edge. Caline placed the twisted sheet in her mother's hands and between her legs and instructed her mother to grip the sheet with her knees and feet. Slowly Caline helped her mother slide over the edge of the roof, making sure she had a good grip on the sheet. "So far, so good!" she said to herself.

She watched as her mother slid slowly down the sheet. Suddenly, there was a gasp. There was no more sheet to hang on to, and her mother fell to the ground.

Caline saw her mother lying on the ground with a surprised look on her face. Then her mother stood up. "I'm okay," she said.

Now it was Caline's turn. She had to get both herself and Miranda safely to the ground. She said to Miranda, "I'm going to sit down on the roof. I want you to climb on my back. Wrap your arms around my neck and your feet around my waist and don't let go until we get to the ground."

Miranda clung so tightly to Caline that she almost choked her. With the sheet under her and a firm grip with both hands, she eased her weight and Miranda's off the edge of the roof. She used her knees and feet to take some of the weight because her arms weren't strong enough. Slowly, they inched their way down the sheet to the end. Her mother was waiting below with both arms outstretched.

There was no more sheet for her feet and knees to grip. Caline couldn't hold on any longer. The two girls went plunging to the ground. Their mother tried but couldn't catch them.

Three bodies and two pillows were in a big heap. One by one the girls and their mother stood up. "We made it! We made it!" they yelled.

The firetruck pulled up, and the firemen saw a house in flames and a mother and two young girls jumping for joy on the front lawn. Someone had called their dad, and he joined them in a family hug.

As Caline's eyes started to close, she smiled at the thought that the tragedy had brought the family closer together than ever before. She couldn't remember a time when her father and mother hugged her with such genuine affection and love.

She had matured today. Her parents looked at her as a brave young lady, not as a kid.

As for Miranda, she seemed to enjoy every minute of the experience. Before Miranda fell asleep in the motel bed that they shared, she said to Caline, "That was fun! Can we do it again real soon?"

Floyd and the Flood

FLOYD AND HIS FAMILY lived in the small town of Beaver Creek in Southern Alberta. Their little frame house was in a beautiful setting. It was on two acres of land that stuck out into the creek. From his upstairs bedroom window, Floyd could look to the right and see the water in the creek bed tumbling over the rocks. To the left there was a wide quiet pool where ducks and geese found a safe haven.

In the summer Floyd swam in the creek and caught some fish off their dock. In the winter he and other kids cleared snow off the ice and made their own hockey rink.

It was now spring. The creek was at a high level with melting snow from the mountains. School had another month to go, and he had to study for the exams that marked the end of the school year.

He was up in his bedroom studying. There were only two bedrooms upstairs. He had one, and his younger sister, Arlene, slept in the other. Their rooms had slanty ceilings like an attic. One side of the room was ten feet high, but by the outside wall it was only five feet high. Floyd heard the rain pounding on the roof, but he had heard rain before and he wasn't concerned.

By 10:00 p.m. he was tired from his studying and was ready for bed. He went downstairs and said, "Good night Mom."

She replied, "Have a good sleep Floyd. I'm pleased that you are studying for your exams."

She and his dad had a bedroom on the main floor. Floyd's dad was a fireman, and he was presently in Northern Alberta fighting forest fires.

Floyd was sleeping soundly. The torrential rain didn't keep him awake. Suddenly, there was a huge crash! He jumped up with a start. It seemed to come from downstairs. He raced downstairs and found water running through the main floor. He went to his parent's bedroom and saw a part of the wall smashed in with water racing through a hole in the wall. His mother had been in bed, and she had been hit by the collapsing wall.

Wading through the fast flowing water, he lifted his mother by the armpits and dragged her upstairs to his room. He checked the other upstairs bedroom, and his baby sister was still sleeping. Floyd knew they had to escape. Soon the whole house would give way to raging waters. He had a window in his room, but it offered no escape route. There was a drop of twenty feet into the flood waters.

The rain had eased up, and he could hear a helicopter overhead. He thought, "If I can only get up on the roof, perhaps I can attract the attention of the helicopter."

The only way out was to break a hole in the roof. He had no axe nor any tools to work with. His bed and dresser were the only furnishings. He took the mattress off his bed and stretched his mother out on it. She was moaning and had a big lump on her head. If only he could get her to a doctor.

With the mattress removed, he looked at his metal bed for a wrecking tool. On each side of the frame was a piece of angle iron connecting the headboard to the footboard. He lifted the angle iron off the frame and used it like a battering ram against the ceiling. The ceiling tiles and insulation came off easily, but he still had to get through the roof boards and shingles.

The iron bar just bounced off the roof boards. He wasn't making any progress. If he didn't get up on the roof, the house and his mother and sister would all be swept away. Then he remembered his lesson in physics. "If I can use the angle iron as a lever, perhaps I can pry some boards loose," he said to himself.

He stood the headboard on its side so it almost touched the low part of the roof. Then he slid the iron bar on top of it so there was a long piece sticking out. (Physics students will know that the headboard was the fulcrum and the angle iron was the lever.)

Floyd grabbed the end of the lever and pulled down with all his weight. The roof planking groaned. Again and again, he threw all his weight on the end of the lever. One plank finally lifted a few inches.

He repositioned the lever to pry up a second plank. The roofing material was holding it back. Using the metal bar as a battering ram, he punched holes in the asphalt roof shingles.

Finally, he climbed on top of the headboard and ripped some of the asphalt shingles with his hands and forced two roofboards upright. There was barely room to squeeze through. He hoisted himself up on the sloping roof. He could see that their house was surrounded by surging muddy water.

Climbing on his hands and knees, he got to the peak of the roof. He sat on the peak with one leg on each side and took off his pajama top and waved it frantically. It was now dawn, and he hoped the helicopter he heard earlier was still around.

Fortunately, a nearby helicopter saw him and headed his way. Floyd said, "Thank you God, but please come quickly."

A chair with a safety harness was lowered from the helicopter and Floyd climbed in. A cable pulled him safely into the helicopter. Floyd was tired from all his exertion and puffed out the words, "My mother and sister are in the upstairs bedrooms. Please save them. There is a small hole in the roof, but you'll need a bigger one to get them out."

A trained rescue operator replied, "Don't worry son. I'll go down and get them out."

The operator was lowered to the roof, and with a fireman's axe he enlarged the hole in the roof. On his first trip he carried up Floyd's mother who was barely conscious. On his next trip he carried up Arlene, who was just starting to wake up.

The rescue operator said to Floyd, "I saw the hole you made in the roof. That was using your head and clever use of the iron bed. You could have all been drowned if you hadn't made it to the roof."

As the helicopter headed for its base on dry land, Floyd looked back and saw their tiny house lifted from its foundations and go tumbling down the swollen creek.

The flooding of Beaver Creek made the National News. Floyd's dad in Northern Alberta was watching the screen anxiously. A camera showed Floyd on the roof top waving to the helicopter. "Hey that's my son!" he shouted to the other firefighters. He jumped up and down as his wife and daughter were brought up. "Thank God they're safe!" he cried out.

As he continued to watch, his house joined the other floating debris in the swollen creek. "Oh no!" he cried. "There goes my house!"

The Football Hero

LIZ LOOKED AT THE TROPHY on her desk for the 1000th time. It was a football player running for a touchdown. The trophy was presented to her brother, and he in turn gave it to her. They shared a special secret, and not even her parents knew their secret.

Liz was the second child with one brother a few years older and one a year younger. Her brothers loved sports, particularly football. When she was six, she kept saying to them, "Throw the ball to me. Throw the ball to me." It was a gentle throw, but she surprised them both by catching it. Once she caught it, she ran away and only her older brother could catch her.

Since that time, they included her in their football practices. She could catch even hard passes and run like a deer. She even played tackle football with a gang of boys. Most of the plays were passing plays. If you could wrap your arms around a receiver or ball carrier, it was considered a tackle, as nobody wore helmets or pads.

Liz was often the receiver, and when she caught the ball the boys seemed eager to wrap their arms around her. They held on to her longer than they might have had she been a boy.

In the city where they lived, there was a Ki-Y league for young boys. It started at 95 pounds with boys around twelve and went to 115 pounds and 135 pounds as they got older. Liz's younger brother, Lionel, who was twelve, played in the 95 pound league. Liz went to see all the games and cheered for her brother and the team. The field where they played was only a half mile from their house, so Lionel changed into his football uniform at home, and he and Liz walked to the playing field.

Lionel's team has made it to the finals. Between games he practiced with Liz and told her the signals and showed her the pass routes he ran. The morning of the final game, he and Liz had a practice session. Lionel was running for a pass, and he stepped in a hole. He fell over in pain. His ankle was severely wrenched. He couldn't walk let alone play football.

"What will the team do?" he cried out. "We have no spares that know how to catch a ball, and they are so slow you could walk faster than they can run."

Lionel looked at Liz. "I've got an idea. You can take my place."

"But it's a boys team," answered Liz.

"With a uniform on, whose going to tell the difference. You're the same size as I am, and the sweater says L. KENNEDY. That's you."

Lionel felt quite proud of himself. Liz was not too sure. She wanted his team to win, but what if she didn't play well, or worse still what if they discovered that she was substituting for her brother.

"Try the uniform on anyway," said Lionel.

Liz took the uniform and pads into her room. She tied up her long blonde hair so it wouldn't show beneath her helmet. For once Liz was glad she didn't have a mature figure which would have spoiled her disguise. In five minutes she came down to the living room to face Lionel.

"I can't believe it. I'm looking at myself. Nobody will ever know the difference. All you have to do is be at the playing field a half hour before game time. You already know the play signals. Tackling might be a problem, but stay low and drive your shoulder into the guy's stomach and wrap your arms around him."

Liz said meekly, "Are you sure I look like you?"

"The spitting image," Lionel replied. "Just go out there and win."

Liz in full football gear joined the other players in warm up before the game. One of Lionel's friends said, "What happened to your sister? She's usually here to root for us."

Liz said, "She has a touch of the flu, but she wishes us good luck."

The boy replied, "Your voice sounds funny. I hope you're not coming down with something."

"I hope not," said Liz, trying to keep her voice as low as possible.

The game started. Liz lined up right at the end, the position Lionel played. It wasn't as easy as she thought. These little kids were rough. The ones she had to block were tough and built low to the ground. On her pass play she ran up ten yards and then broke to the sidelines. The defence seemed to read her mind, and a speedy little guy was always beside her. In the huddle she whispered hoarsely to the quarterback, "I think I can fake going to the side and go straight down the field."

"Okay we'll give it a try," he said.

Liz ran her usual pattern and made a move to the side. The

defensive back cut sideways, but she continued downfield. There was a ball coming towards her. Normally, she caught even the hardest pass, but she wasn't used to the shoulder pads. The ball bounced off her pads. She was forced to juggle it. Finally, she pulled it into her chest. Then, with all the speed she could muster, she raced for the goal line. The crowd cheered. She had a touchdown.

The quarterback slapped her on the back. "Great work Lionel! I've never seen you run so fast."

The game see-sawed back and forth. The other team scored a touchdown, and it was tied at seven all. With less than a minute left, Liz's team kicked the ball to their opponent's five-yard line. The fastest boy on the other team cut back over his goal line intending to go around Liz. If she missed him, he could go all the way for a touchdown. He faked to the inside and went around the outside. He was almost past her. In desperation, she threw herself sideways intending to grab his ankles. She missed and his heel came up and split her lip. She could taste the blood and felt like crying as she lay on the ground.

All of a sudden, her teammates were helping her to her feet and whacking her helmet. Her contact caused the runner to trip and fall. Their team had scored a safety touch for two points. They went on to win the game by a score of 9 to 7.

All the players went back to the locker room to change and talk about their victory. Liz had to go to the bathroom badly. Without saying a word, she ran home. On her way to the bathroom, she passed Lionel in the kitchen. "We won!" she yelled out.

Later, she had time to tell Lionel all the details of the game. He was very proud of her and was sympathetic about her split lip. She didn't feel any pain because the joy of the victory had erased it.

One week later, the team had a big celebration banquet. Lionel was voted the most valuable player and was presented with a beautiful trophy. He hobbled up in his crutches with his ankle still swollen.

"What happened to you?" his coach said.

"I ran home from the game to tell Liz that we had won, and I stepped in a hole and sprained my ankle," Lionel said with a straight face.

"Well I see your lip healed all right. You kissed that guy right where it hurt — on his heel."

Lionel left the banquet feeling guilty. He presented the trophy to Liz as soon as he got home. It was a secret they shared for all of their lives. There never was a closer bond between brother and sister.

Robber for Sale

MATTHEW LOVED PLAYING SOCCER. It wasn't as rough a sport as hockey or football. He had a slim build and preferred running to bodily contact. He was skilled at dribbling the ball and at side stepping opponents who tried to block him.

A technique he hadn't perfected was kicking the ball. His passes to his teammates were often inaccurate. His shooting on goal was usually off the mark. If he kicked it too hard, it would sail out of the park, and if he tried a controlled kick it dribbled to the goalie.

Tonight, he was playing for his school. His parents were regular supporters but had to miss the game as they volunteered to take part in a one-night blitz for a national charity. He would miss their cheers.

His team was leading 1 to 0, thanks to one of his better kicks. He saw another opportunity. The ball was passed to him but five feet in front of him. He raced to intercept it, but a player from the other team had the same idea. There was a big collision. Matthew, who was a slimmer build, was knocked down.

Matthew's teammate also arrived on the scene. He pulled his

right foot back to kick the ball. Matthew's head was suddenly on the ground in front of the ball. The kicker couldn't stop his foot in mid-air.

The thud could be heard in the stands. Matthew not only heard it, but he felt it. The boot connected with the left side of his face. First, he saw all the stars in the heaven only a foot from his face. Next, he saw only half the stars, as his left eye had closed. He felt his face. His eye had a mound above and below it. His cheekbone had a walnut sized lump.

The referee, his coach and the players all converged on Matthew. "Are you all right?" his coach asked.

Matthew sat up. His face was sore, but his mind was clear. He bravely said, "It probably looks worse than it is."

His coach said, "If you can make it home, I suggest you put some ice on it right away. That will reduce the swelling."

Matthew got to his feet, collected his belongings, and headed home only a few blocks away. He knew his mother would make a big fuss over his swollen eye. He was brave whenever he got hurt, but sympathy from his mother usually brought on his tears.

He went in the front door, expecting to see his parents, but he was met by a strange man. He looked in the kitchen, and there were his mom and dad both gagged and tightly bound to kitchen chairs.

The strange man spoke up, "Okay son, you're just in time. Pull up a chair, and I'll tie you up with your parents."

Matthew was in shock, but he had to outsmart the robber. "I'm not staying in this house any longer," he cried out. "Look what my dad did to me. He's always beating me."

The robber looked at Matthew's face. "Why, that's awful," he said.

"What kind of father would beat his son like that?"

Matthew interrupted. "I thought they would be still out canvassing. I came back to get a few clothes, and then I was going to run away. Will you take me with you?"

The robber was genuinely upset with the beating Matthew had taken. "The best I can do is drop you off on the highway. Let's go if you're coming."

Matthew said, "I'll just grab a small bag. I won't be a second."

Matthew ran to his room, grabbed a small gym bag and threw in a few clothes. He saw a stick-on FOR SALE sign he intended to use to help sell his old bike and stuck it in his gym bag.

"Okay, Let's go!" he said.

Taking one last look at his parents, he saw a look of disbelief and fright on their faces. They were more concerned about Matthew than the loss of all their money and valuables.

Matthew got in the passenger side of the robber's car. He noticed that the licence plate was muddy, and he couldn't make out any numbers or letters. The swollen side of his face was on the robber's side, and he could sense the robber's sympathy.

They proceeded through town and came to a stop at the last light before the highway. "This will be fine," Matthew said.

Before the robber could reply, Matthew hopped out of the car. He waved as the car and its driver sped off down the highway.

Matthew knew the police station was only a block away. He raced there as fast as he could.

The policeman at the counter gasped when he saw a young boy, whose face was all swollen up, come dashing in the door.

"Help! Help!" Matthew cried out. "A robber has tied up my parents and is headed out of town on Highway No. 10."

"Did you get the licence plate and car description?" asked the nearest policeman.

"The car is a brown Plymouth, about five years old. The licence plate was all covered with mud, and I couldn't read the number, but there is a big FOR SALE sign stuck on the passenger door. The robber doesn't know it's there."

"Okay son, we'll get right on it," replied the policeman. "Where do you live so we can take you home?"

Matthew got in the police cruiser and felt very important. In five minutes, they were at his home. His parents were still tied to their chairs and making moaning noises with tape covering their mouths.

As soon as they were cut free from the ropes and had the tape removed, Matthew's dad said, "What's this about my beating you, and where's the robber?"

Matthew replied, "I got hurt playing soccer. I made up the story to fool the robber. He is on the highway right now with the police on his tail."

The policeman took a report from Matthew's mother listing the money and valuables that were stolen. He was about to leave when his beeper went off. "Excuse me a minute," he said.

He went out to his car and came back with a smile on his face. "We have caught your robber, and you should recover all your money and stolen goods. Thanks to your son for putting the FOR SALE sign on the side of the car. Sorry about the robbery, and don't forget to put ice on that eye."

"Oh you poor dear," Matthew's mother said. "We have done nothing about your eye. It must be very painful. Let me kiss it and make it better."

With that, the hero of the day was reduced to tears.

French Fries

TANYA HURRIED HOME from school. She wanted to be with her mother who was expecting her third child any day. Her mother insisted on doing everything herself even though she had a two-year-old little girl under her feet.

Tanya burst in the door and yelled, "Hi Mom!"

"Hi dear! You're just in time to help me set the table."

The smell of French fries in boiling oil filled the room. It was a delightful aroma that made your mouth water. Tanya's mother was setting the table. She had four dinner plates held out at arm's length to clear her extended stomach. She took two steps and suddenly clutched her stomach and cried out in pain.

She crumpled to the floor and the plates went crashing down with pieces scattered over the whole dining area.

Tanya cried out "Mother! Mother!" and went rushing to her side. Her mother was moaning and curled up on the floor with her knees gathered up in front of her. Tanya put a small pillow under her mother's head and wondered what she should do. Out of the corner of her eye she saw flames at the stove. The oil had boiled over on to the red-hot element. The pot of french fries was a flaming inferno.

Quickly, Tanya grabbed oven mitts, turned off the element, and raced to get a pot lid to put on the pot of burning oil. She knew enough not to splash water on the oil.

The lid snuffed out the flames in the pot, but the top of the stove was covered with little fires as the oil had splattered out of the pot. Tanya wet a big towel and squeezed it out so it wasn't dripping and dragged it slowly over the top of the stove. It smothered the little pockets of flames and picked up most of the hot oil on the surface.

The flames were now all out. There was smoke in the room, but it wasn't hurting anyone. She looked at her mother still moaning on the floor; then she glanced at her sister Manda across the room. She was playing with blocks unaware of the fire and her mother's collapse. All around Manda were broken pieces of china. She could easily pick one up and cut her hand or worse still put a piece in her mouth.

Tanya stepped between the pieces of broken china and picked up Manda. She strapped her in a high chair and even gave her a cookie to stop any complaints. The floor was covered with little bits of china. It took Tanya a few minutes to sweep it all up and put the mess in the garbage pail.

With emergencies under control, she knelt down beside her mother, who was moaning and had her eyes half closed. Tanya didn't know what to do. She thought of calling 911, but her dad would be home soon. They probably had a room at the hospital reserved, but Tanya didn't know anything about their plans.

Her dad would have left the office. It was after 5:00 p.m. The lady next door was not their closest friend, but maybe she would help. Tanya wasn't big enough to lift her mother and wasn't old enough to know what mothers go through before a baby is born.

Tanya picked up the phone and dialed Mrs. Watt. "Mrs. Watt, this is Tanya next door. My mother just collapsed on the kitchen floor. I think her baby is due, and I need help to get her into bed."

"Stay with her dear, and I'll be right there," Mrs. Watt excitedly replied.

The front door opened, and an alarmed Mrs. Watt rushed into the kitchen. She stroked Tanya's mother's hair and spoke to her softly. Then she said to Tanya, "Your mother had a severe pain and more will follow. She will need to go to the hospital, but a half hour of rest shouldn't hurt. Do you think you can help me to get her to bed?"

Tanya got on one side and Mrs. Watt on the other and they helped Tanya's mother to her feet. Taking most of her weight, they made their way slowly to the bedroom and stretched her out on her own bed.

"You go down and look after your sister, and I'll make sure your mother is comfortable," Mrs. Watt instructed Tanya.

By this time, Manda had finished her cookie and was getting impatient in her high chair. Tanya gave her another cookie, turned on the fan above the stove to get rid of the smoke, and opened the back door for fresh air. Her dad would be home soon, and she didn't want him to see the messy stove.

With strong detergent, she wiped it clean and checked the rest of the kitchen for broken china. Satisfied all was in order, she joined Manda with a cookie and a glass of milk.

She heard her dad's car. "Thank goodness!" she thought.

"Where's Mom?" were her dad's first words when he came in the door.

"She had a bad pain and is lying down. Mrs. Watt is with her."

Tanya's dad rushed out of the kitchen to join his wife. Tanya overheard him call the doctor, and then there was a lot of scurrying as bags were packed and preparations were made to drive to the hospital. Her dad dashed from room to room and seemed to forget what he went for.

Mrs. Watt came into the kitchen. "I've offered to take you and Manda over to my place until your dad gets home. I'm sure your mother will be fine. After all, she had you and Manda and everything turned out all right. My family are expecting supper so we better go now."

They all went next door to Mrs. Watt's. She had the table all set. A roast was cooking in the oven. "My husband likes french fries, but I don't think I will cook them tonight. The boiling oil is too dangerous with little children around. I suggest you and Manda go in the den and watch TV. Looking after the stove and having babies are not jobs for children."

The Hitchhiker

DANNY LOVED PLAYING HOCKEY. Twice a week his dad took him to the local rink. It was more fun for Danny than for his dad who had to do the driving. Today was typical Calgary winter weather; it was only –30 degrees Celsius. Blowing snow made driving hazardous, and only the main roads were plowed. There were warnings on TV and on the radio telling residents to dress warmly as the wind chill factor made it even colder.

Danny was happy. He played well today, and they had won their exhibition game. He stood at the door of the rink with his equipment bag waiting for his dad to pick him up. He spotted his family's blue Ford and waved to his dad.

His dad opened the front door and said, "Hop in son. How did it go tonight?"

"We won," said Danny. "And I got two goals."

"That's terrific," replied his dad.

There were just about to pull away when Danny's dad noticed an older boy standing, half freezing, near the door of the rink. He stuck his thumb out, hoping to get a ride. He had his equipment bag and hockey stick but no hat or gloves, and his light jacket was not meant for –30 degree weather.

"I should give this kid a ride to the nearest bus stop," his dad said. "It's a bad night to be standing out in the cold."

Danny's father pulled the car over to where the boy was standing and said, "Do you want to ride to the nearest bus stop?"

The boy very politely said, "Thank you sir." He climbed in the back seat with his hockey gear.

They got out on the road and Danny's father said, "And where can I take you?"

The voice from the back said, "Edmonton."

This was the 300 km to the north. Danny's father turned his head in surprise and locked into the muzzle of a gun. He had no choice but to head the car towards Edmonton.

In the front seat, Danny wondered what he could do to overcome the hitchhiker. He was much bigger than Danny and, with the gun pointed at the back of his dad's head, there didn't seem like much Danny could do.

They were several miles north of Calgary when Danny said to his dad, "Did you bring my insulin kit for my diabetes?"

"No son, it's at home. We thought you'd be home by now."

Danny said, "I feel an attack coming on. A chocolate bar could ward it off."

Danny's father half-turned to the boy in the back and said, "If he gets an attack, he will be thrashing all over the front seat like a mad man. I will need to stop the car and get medical attention. If we can stop and get him his chocolate bar, we can buy some time."

The boy in the back knew nothing about a diabetic attack, but it sounded very serious to him. He said, "We can stop at the next gas station. Your son can get out. He is not to say a word. He must stay away from a phone. He is to pay for the chocolate bar and leave. If not you get this bullet, and I'll take the car."

In about 15 minutes, they came to a service station. Danny got out with a two-dollar bill. He picked out his chocolate bar, put the two-dollar bill on the counter and walked out.

In the car, he proceeded to eat the chocolate bar and muttered, "Thanks." The armed hitchhiker was pleased that the boy had followed his instructions. He was worried that the boy might have tried to be a hero which could have caused an ugly situation.

Back at the gas station, the attendant picked up the two-dollar bill. "The kid didn't even wait for his change," he said to himself. When he picked up the two dollars, there was a little piece of paper under it. Printed on the paper were the words "Help, armed hitchhiker, Blue Ford, M0X 510."

The attendant immediately called the police.

Meanwhile, Danny, his father and the hitchhiker were cruising along the highway towards Edmonton. "There looks to be some commotion up ahead," said Danny's father.

As they approached the flashing lights, he realized it was a roadblock. He was forced to stop. In a parked police car beside the roadblock, four policemen jumped out with their guns pointed at the windows of their car.

"Everybody out, with your hands up," an officer shouted. All three tumbled out and had to place their hands on the roof of the car. They were searched, and the police found the loaded gun in the pocket of the hitchhiker. They immediately slapped the handcuffs on him.

"Let's see what he's got in the bag," the policeman said. The bag was emptied. It wasn't hockey equipment. It was full of trophies from the rink, wallets and watches belonging to the players and new hockey sweaters from the gift shop.

Danny and his father were just as surprised as the police. The coaches had repeatedly warned the players not to bring valuables and money to the rink as lockers had been broken into before.

"You folks can go now," said the policeman to Danny and his father. "Thank you for your help. We'll be in touch with you soon."

Before they left, Danny's father asked if they had a phone to call Calgary. His wife would be worried that they weren't back from the rink. He called and said they had a slight delay and would be home in an hour.

On their way home, Danny's father said, "How did you invent that diabetes' story? And good work with the note, I'm glad our passenger in the back didn't notice."

Danny replied, "A friend of mine has diabetes, and it was the best reason I could think of to stop. By the way, could you stop at the gas station so I can get my change?"

His dad said, "Son, they deserve a tip. Here is two dollars to replace yours. I think it was money well spent. I hope you enjoyed your chocolate bar."

Horseshoe Harry

TWO YEARS AGO, Harry and his family moved from a city house to a ranch only ten miles from the city. The ranch was in the foothills of the Rocky Mountains, and they could see the mountains as well as the city lights. Harry's dad always wanted to have a property and to own a horse. Harry was happy living in the city, but he didn't have a choice in the move.

He missed playing road hockey with the kids on the street. He longed to walk a block to the local grocery store where he could buy bubble gum and baseball cards. There were many things he missed about life in the city. The nearest ranch was a mile away, and the neighbouring kids weren't his age.

Harry's dad knew the boy would be lonely and spent as much time as he could with him. He built a horseshoe pit and taught Harry how to throw horseshoes. At first Harry couldn't pitch the horseshoe anywhere near the pegs. His dad said, "Hold the horseshoe on the side with the points down. When it hits the dirt, it will dig in and not slide. In this game the pegs are always forty feet apart. Once you find the range, practice the same shot."

Harry practiced when his dad was away. He found the range,

but often the shoe came in backwards and banged off the peg. He tried giving the shoe a little spin. With a twist of the wrist, he could control the number of times the horseshoe turned before it reached the peg. Soon he could throw the shoe so it landed prongs first and slid around the peg for a ringer.

Harry challenged his dad to a match. His dad agreed to the challenge certain that he would beat Harry. He knew Harry liked the game, and he didn't want to discourage him by beating him too badly. Of course, the opposite happened. Harry beat his dad. It was almost no contest.

"Congratulations son! You've certainly improved your game." Harry's dad was proud of his son, but he was a little put out that Harry beat him so badly.

Harry brought friends home from school, and his dad often invited business friends to the ranch. It wasn't long before the subject of horseshoes came up. Every visitor was sure he could beat Harry. They didn't stand a chance.

Harry's skill at horseshoe was soon recognized in the community. He was nicknamed "Horseshoe Harry."

One day, Harry's dad drove in the yard pulling a horse-trailer. Harry went out to investigate. "I just bought a very expensive colt. He's going to be yours to ride and possibly race someday," said Harry's dad proudly.

Harry's jaw dropped. He didn't know what to say. Something happened to his knees. They suddenly felt weak. The colt was beautiful. Harry couldn't help but fall in love with her. They called her "Candy" because she was so sweet.

In the next few months, Harry spent every available moment grooming Candy and riding her around their track. He would have liked to sleep in the same stall as Candy, but his parents wouldn't allow it.

Harry no longer wanted to move back to the city. His love for Candy and his fame at being the local champion horseshoe player were two big reasons why he loved life on the ranch.

Harry usually slept soundly once he went to bed, but one night he had a restless sleep. He heard the clock strike every hour. Shortly after two in the morning, he heard the sound of a car motor and car doors shutting. Out of curiosity he went out to investigate. There was a strange car with a horse-trailer parked outside their barn. He was first startled then raging mad when he saw two men leading Candy to a horse-trailer. They were stealing his horse.

There wasn't time for him to run to his parents. The thieves would be gone before he and his parents could get back. He had to do something. Ten feet away were two horseshoes ringed around the peg. He picked them up and ran around the side of the barn so the thieves couldn't see him.

He came to the corner of the barn and poked his head around. They were about to lead Candy up the ramp to the trailer. He judged the distance. It was about two yards further than the regulation forty feet between horseshoe pegs. He took two giant steps. The thieves were too busy to notice.

With a well-practiced motion, he pitched a horseshoe at the thief on the right. There was a dull thud; then a scream. The horseshoe had circled his ankle. Next Harry threw a second shoe at the other thief. There was a solid clunk, and the thief fell over in pain grabbing his ankle.

Harry didn't want them to escape. He ran up and took the rope they used to lead Candy and tied up the helpless thieves. He saw the pain on their faces and knew they couldn't run far even if they did untie the ropes.

Then he took Candy back to her stall and ran to get his parents. At two in the morning, they took a minute to come to their senses. Dressed in housecoats, they stumbled after Harry to the yard and saw the strange car and the horse-trailer. But the strangest sight of all was that of two grown men crying, all trussed up in a rope.

Harry's dad called the police who came and took the thieves, the car and the horse-trailer away. When the police undid the rope, they found the thieves couldn't stand up or walk. They each had a broken right ankle.

The senior policeman came up to Harry. "Those were very accurate tosses son. You must be an expert at horseshoes."

"Thank you, Sir. I wasn't that good. My second throw wasn't a ringer. The shoe came in backwards. I think I lost my composure. If it had been a tournament, I would have only one point instead of three and likely lost. I'm just happy that I could do something to stop them from stealing Candy. She is the most wonderful thing that ever happened to me."

Stay Off the Ice

BACK IN 1812, two Grenadiers fell through the ice and drowned in the pond. The soldiers named it Grenadier Pond. Mike and Cliff didn't know the history of the pond which was considered bottomless, but they felt its icy waters and without help they could have been its latest victims.

Grenadier Pond is in the west end of Toronto. Over the years thousands of boys and girls have skated on the pond. Toboggans have slid across its width, starting with a toboggan slide on the east side or the High Park side.

In the spring, summer and fall, Tod, Mike and Cliff had all of High Park as their playground. They fished in the pond, and Mike got a prize for the second biggest fish caught. They enjoyed playing hide and go seek with their friends and felt like the park was their own backyard.

One Saturday morning in late November, the weather was below freezing, but the pond was not considered safe. Signs all around the shore warned skaters to stay off the ice. In a few weeks they would have their own rinks on the frozen ice surface, but now was not the time.

Tod lived in a big house facing the pond. His friend Mike and Cliff lived a block away. Today, they gathered at Tod's to play road hockey.

It was Cliff who smelled it first. Someone was setting up a hotdog stand beside the toboggan slides. It was too early in the season to toboggan, but many people walked through the park and hot dogs and hamburgers were inviting on a cold day.

The smell of fried onions and barbecued hot dogs drifted across the pond. Cliff said, "I've got some money from shovelling snow. I'd love a hot dog."

Mike was in agreement. "My mouth is watering. I can almost taste the fried onions."

It was Tod who held back. "You know you can't walk on the ice. It's too dangerous. At breakfast this morning my mother said, 'Remember to stay off the ice!'"

Cliff had all the answers. "Those signs have been up for weeks. It's much colder now. Besides, we don't weigh much. Let's go Mike."

Mike didn't want Cliff to call him "chicken" so he joined him, and two of the three nine year olds headed across the pond. Tod stood on the shore and watched.

They seemed to be doing fine until they came to a section of blue ice. The thin ice cracked, and both of the boys went into the freezing water. Cliff and Mike couldn't touch bottom, and when they tried to climb out, the thin sheet of ice cracked with their weight.

On the shore, Tod knew he had to do something. There wasn't time to run for help. Leaning against the back wall of their house was an old five-seater toboggan. The long cushion was missing and the curved boards were cracked, but he knew the toboggan would spread his weight over the ice.

He grabbed the toboggan and dashed for the shoreline. Then he dove headfirst with the toboggan under him. It coasted on the ice more than halfway to his friends. Rather than step on the ice, he paddled the toboggan with his arms.

Cliff was the nearest. Tod spun the toboggan around so Cliff could climb up on the tail end of it. Cliff crawled to the front to make room for Mike to climb on. Tod supported his shoulders on the curved front of the toboggan and spread his legs out on the ice. Cliff helped pull Mike up, but it took a few tries because the ice kept crumbling.

Finally, all three boys were on the toboggan. They used their hands on each side to push it toward the shore. In a frightened tone, Cliff said to Tod, "Don't tell my mother. She told me not to go on the pond."

Mike said, "Me too. She warned me to stay off the ice."

Tod said, "I'll keep your secret, but you can't go home like that. Come to my house, and I'll give you some dry clothes to wear home."

The three boys quietly entered the back door of Tod's house and tip toed to his bedroom. Mike and Cliff took off their dripping clothes, and Tod looked in his drawers and closet for something they could wear.

Tod managed to find some old clothes that fit his friends. He gave them each a plastic bag to carry their wet clothes.

Mike and Cliff took off for home, pleased that their parents were unaware that the boys had fallen through the ice. Tod pledged to keep their secret.

It was Sunday morning. His dad was reading the morning paper, and Tod glanced over his shoulder. There was a picture of a boy in the paper, and Tod thought it looked just like him. Then he read the headlines.

"HEROIC RESCUE OF TWO BOYS ON GRENADIER POND"

Tod's dad looked up and said, "Well Tod, what's this all about?"

There wasn't much to tell. A witness to the rescue, who was out bird watching in High Park, focused his telephoto lens on Tod and the boys in the icy water. The first picture was of Tod making his way on the toboggan towards Mike and Cliff. The second showed Tod helping the two boys into the toboggan and the third caught Tod and the two dripping wet boys running towards Tod's house.

The photographer didn't know who the three boys were, but he knew he had a great story. However, the identity of the boys was soon known. Mike's and Cliff's adventure or misadventure was no longer a secret. Tod was acclaimed in the next issue of the paper as the local hero.

Mike and Cliff got a stern lecture from their parents, particularly since they had been told to stay off the ice. The newspaper established a scholarship fund for Tod, and the readers gave generously. When interviewed by the paper, Tod was modest and shy. He said the rescue was the least he could do for his friends.

Poison Ivy

RICK FOUND THE treasure of treasures. He couldn't believe his eyes. He was looking for an extra paddle in the basement of their cottage and moved some boxes that had been there for years. At his feet was a six-quart wicker basket full of lead soldiers. If happiness is floating in the air, Rick was several feet off the ground. He had heard how his grandfather loved playing with soldiers, and these must have belonged to his grandpa.

Rick looked with amazement at the colourful uniforms. There were the famous British Redcoats, Grenadiers, Beef Eaters, armoured knights, charging cavalry, and infantrymen and artillery dating back to the first World War.

With the basket of soldiers in one hand, Rick raced to a wooded area in front of their cottage. He was the army general. He had to prepare his defences before the land attack came. He dug trenches, set up barricades and placed soldiers in strategic positions. It was war, but to Rick it was more like heaven.

The battle scene was interrupted when Rick got a call for supper. He excitedly told his parents about the treasure he had found. They agreed that the soldiers were originally Grandpa's, but they saw no reason why Rick couldn't play with them.

That night Rick went to bed with a smile he couldn't hide. He had new plans for his fortifications. The defensive positions would be the envy of other army generals.

He woke up in the morning anxious to set up the battle-lines, but his hands had a strange itch and tiny water blisters were forming. He showed them to his mother.

"Why you have poison ivy," she exclaimed. "You must have dug around some roots when you were making those trenches. We have some liquid that's good for poison ivy. It's called 'tincture of iron'. It will stain your hands brown, but it dries the water blisters."

Rick ended up with a brown stain over his hands. He had orders to stay away from his fortifications and that particular wooded area. Fortunately, Rick was well tanned so the brown stain wasn't too obvious.

The Saturday after he got poison ivy, he had to stay home while his parents went shopping. He was in the cottage when a man came to the door. He said he was from an insurance company, and he needed to appraise the contents of the cottage to complete an insurance policy. Rick let him in and followed him around to make sure he didn't take anything.

When the man was leaving, he thanked Rick and grabbed his hand to shake it. It was too late for Rick to tell him he could get poison ivy by shaking hands.

The next day Rick and his parents went to a regatta with boat races and summer activities. As usual they didn't lock the cottage. Nobody locked the doors to summer cottages unless they were closing up for the winter. When they returned, they were shocked. The TV, VCR, silverware and expensive ornaments were missing.

They checked with the neighbours and, fortunately, one of them had seen a suspicious looking truck parked in their driveway and had written down the licence number. The neighbour hadn't seen the driver, but the licence number was a big help.

Rick and his parents went to the police. The police traced the licence number and found that the man who owned the truck lived only a few miles down the main road. The police, Rick, and his parents went to the thief's house and knocked on the door. When the man came to the door, Rick cried out: "That's the insurance man!"

Of course, the man denied ever having been near the cottage. The police said, "It's his word against your son's. Unless you've got more proof, we can't arrest him."

Rick frowned. His shoulders slumped. The man was going to get away with his crime. Suddenly, Rick smiled. His shoulders straightened and he said, "He shook hands with me, and I bet he has poison ivy on his right hand." The man was forced to show his right hand and sure enough it was covered with a poison ivy rash.

The man confessed to his crime, and the police found all the stolen property. Rick's father was upset because Rick let the man in the house to examine the contents, but he couldn't get too angry because it was Rick's poison ivy that was the important clue in capturing the robber.

Kidnapped

"KIKI, YOUR BREAKFAST is ready," Anna the maid called out.

Anna had already prepared breakfast for Kiki's dad, Judge Edwin Spencer and her mother, Dr. Elizabeth Spencer.

"Coming," was Kiki's reply.

When she sat down at the breakfast table, the judge was finishing his coffee and reading the financial section of the paper. He put down his paper and looked directly at Kiki.

"I'm worried about your going to school without an adult. There are some crazy people out there and you're still a little girl."

"Nonsense Dad. I'm in grade 3, not in kindergarten anymore. All the kids in grade 3 walk to school on their own. If I had a parent or nanny with me, all the kids would tease me."

"Nevertheless," the judge replied. "There is a real danger, and we want to make sure you're safe. Perhaps my chauffeur could drop you off before he takes me to work."

"That would be way too early, and the kids would make fun of me even more," Kiki replied.

"You should listen to your father. He's only saying what's best for you," her mother answered in defence of her husband.

A faint honk of a horn was heard. "That's Mike with the limousine. I have to go now, but we'll continue the conversation tonight." The judge put on his coat, picked up his briefcase and walked out to the chauffeur driven limousine.

Kiki finished her breakfast and bundled up for the cold winter weather. "Bye Mom, bye Anna. See you later. I don't want to be late for school."

"You take care dear," called out her mother, who was getting ready to go to the nearby medical clinic where she was head of staff.

Kiki walked down the street and was soon joined by her classmate, Kathy. The two eight-year-olds chatted away as they walked to the school. A dark blue car parked at the curb was of no interest to them.

As Kiki was about to walk past the car, the back door opened and a man jumped out. He grabbed Kiki and threw her on the floor in the back of the car. He tossed a car blanket over her head and put his feet on top of her shoulders.

Kathy was knocked to the ground but not hurt. She realized what happened to Kiki, and she ran back to Kiki's mansion-like house. Anna answered the door.

"Help! Help! Kiki's been kidnapped!" Kathy cried out.

Poor Anna! She had to call Kiki's parents and the police. Within twenty minutes the judge, Kiki's mom and a police officer were gathered in the living room of the big house.

The police officer spoke up. "You will probably get a call for ransom money within the hour. They will ask you to drive alone to some secluded spot. I will lie down on the floor with a periscope to watch out for the kidnapper. I will be in radio contact with an unmarked car which will follow us. Agree to the money, but don't give them all they ask. A box full of small bills looks like a huge amount, and the kidnapper can't add it up on the spot."

Meanwhile, Kiki lay in the back of the car, scared but not hurt. She thought if she struggled or screamed, she might get hurt. She knew the car was driving through the city, stopping at lights and stop signs. Then it picked up speed as if driving on the highway. Suddenly, it slowed and went down a bumpy country road.

The car stopped. The man wrapped Kiki up in the blanket and carried her into the house. He put a pillowcase over her head and tied her to a chair. All she saw were his hands. He was white with big strong hands. One finger had a gold signet ring with the letter "G".

The man spoke up. "Good driving Daisie. I have to go to a public phone booth to make a call. By tonight we will be rich. Be back in half an hour."

"Okay Gus. I'll look after the millionaire's brat."

At the Spencer home, the judge and police officer were awaiting the call. When the phone rang, they each picked up a phone.

A muffled voice said, "I have your daughter. If you want her returned, you do exactly as I say. Drive to the camping site on highway 10 just outside the city. It is deserted this time of year. Leave 500 hundred thousand dollars in a briefcase on the floor in the phone booth. Come alone at three p.m. on the dot. If you don't follow these instructions, you will never see your daughter again." The caller hung up before the judge could reply.

While the kidnapper was making his call, Kiki sat quietly tied to a chair. She didn't bother speaking to the woman called Daisie.

A door opened and shut. The kidnapper had returned. "By three p.m. we'll have half a million dollars. What an easy way to make money. There is one little problem. A young girl with Kiki could have seen the car. Rather than take it to the rendezvous, we'll have to take the R.V. We can lock Kiki in the bathroom, throw her out after we get the money and then take off on our vacation."

Daisie eagerly added, "I can't wait to spend some of that money on the beaches in Florida."

Sometime in the afternoon, Kiki was carried out to the R.V. and pushed into the bathroom. She heard the bathroom door being locked. She pulled off the pillowcase and looked around. There was a small window, but it had frosted glass and was locked or jammed shut. At the bottom edge of the window frame, ice had formed. She thought, "If I can melt the ice, maybe there will be a crack at the bottom."

Kiki took a face cloth and soaked in hot water and lay it repeatedly on the layer of ice. Soon the ice was gone, but the crack was only as wide as a dime.

The R.V. was now on the highway. Somehow, she had to tell someone that she was kidnapped.

In the medicine cabinet there were two safety pins and a tube of lipstick. She pulled out some toilet paper and printed with lipstick:

H

E

L

P

K

I

K

I

The R.V. had stopped. She must act now. She fastened the safety pins to the edge of the toilet paper and fed it through the slot. Then she prayed that someone would see it.

Five or ten minutes went by, and all was quiet. Then she heard, "Get out with your hands up! Hands on top of the roof!"

Footsteps approached the bathroom door. A police officer opened the door and said, "Are you all right Kiki?"

She didn't know what to say, so she just hugged him.

Stepping out of the R.V., she saw a big man with a gold signet ring in handcuffs. By his side was a middle-aged woman, also in handcuffs.

Her dad came running over to her. Tearfully he said, "Thank God you're safe! Thank God you're safe!"

"You were a very smart girl to think of a way to tell us where you were. The police officer in the back of my car spotted your sign and had his back-up cruiser make the arrest. Your mother is anxiously waiting at home. We had better phone her right now."

"By the way, is there anything you need? You weren't hurt were you?"

"Well, I did miss out on lunch. Do you think Anna could make some macaroni and cheese, and could I have some ice cream for dessert?"

www.ingramcontent.com/pod-product-compliance
Lightning Source LLC
Chambersburg PA
CBHW020239030726
47497CB00009B/3169